# I Am a Good Friend:
# Helping Kids Understand Friendship

## The "I Am" Series, Book 2

By
Belle Green

With
Sheri Moroe

Illustrated by
Maruf Hasan

Be sure to check out Book 1 in this series, too!

*I Am Good in My Heart: Helping Kids Understand Self-Worth*

## About Belle

Belle Green is a lifelong writer specializing in inspirational fiction and nonfiction and children's books. She lives outside of Atlanta, Georgia with her husband and son. Belle is the youngest of nine children and has 23 nieces and nephews and 16 great nieces and nephews.

## About Sheri

Sheri Moroe is a behavior specialist that has worked with children for more than 30 years. Sheri has a BS in Early Childhood Development, a Masters in Clinical Psychology and is currently pursuing her doctorate in Clinical Mental Health. She has worked with a wide range of children with developmental delay, autism as well as typical behavior issues. She has three grown children of her own and a beautiful grandson. She has a continuing passion to help children and adults learn a more positive way to modify unwanted behaviors.

Dear Parent or Caregiver,

Thank you for choosing this book! Entering the world of friendships can be challenging for young children who are still in the process of developing empathy and tend to view their experiences only from their own perspective. It can be difficult for them to understand their own feelings and the feelings of their playmates. We hope that *I Am a Good Friend* will help your child understand the behaviors and feelings that we all have in healthy friendships and make positive choices that are good for everyone.

Blessings,

Belle Green
&
Sheri Moroe

I am a good friend! Friends are so much fun!

Good friends like to share. Sometimes I forget, and I don't want to share my toys.

But my friend feels sad if I don't share,
and no one is having any fun.

It's important for me to remember that I am
a good friend, all the time, every time!
Good friends know that everyone has
more fun when we share our toys.

Sometimes my friend wants to play outside, but I want to do a puzzle. I want it my way!

But it's not as fun to play inside alone, and my friend isn't having as much fun either.

It's important for me to remember that I am
a good friend, all the time, every time.
Good friends know that everyone has
more fun when we use our imaginations together.

Sometimes my friend and I want to play
with the same toy at the same time. I want it!

But if I take it my friend doesn't have a toy
and it's not as much fun to play alone.

It's important for me to remember that I am
a good friend, all the time, every time!
Good friends know that everyone has
more fun when we take turns with our toys.

Sometimes my friend wants to do something without asking first...and sometimes I might want to do it, too!

But I know we will get in trouble, then my friend might have to go home and we can't play anymore.

It's important for me to remember that I am
a good friend, all the time, every time!
Good friends know that we can play together longer
when we make good choices and ask for things first.

Sometimes I have a friend with an allergy who can't eat a food that I like. But I want to eat it now!

If I eat it now in front of my friend, she might get sick.
I need to wait until my friend is safe.

It's important for me to remember that I am
a good friend, all the time, every time!
Good friends know that they should eat safe foods
together. I can have my other snack later.

Sometimes my friend has an owie and it looks funny.
Some kids laugh at her. I want to fit in!

But if I make fun of my friend it hurts her feelings and she cries. I don't want to make my friend cry and feel sad. I want to make my friend feel good!

It's important for me to remember that I am
a good friend, all the time, every time!
Good friends know that making someone cry
is wrong – it's time to tell a grown up.

Sometimes I am playing with
friends and we are having fun,
but then something happens
and I stop playing.

When a friend stops playing it means it's time for everyone to stop playing and find out what's wrong. They might be hurt or sick.

It's important for me to remember that I am
a good friend, all the time, every time!
Good friends make sure that everyone is having fun.
Sometimes good friends need to get a grown up to help.

Good friends care about each other and want everyone to be happy. They know that getting along is more important than toys.

Good friends think
about each other.

Good friends know that being together
is more important than who goes first.

When I remember that I am a good friend,
it makes play time so much more fun!
I feel great about being me!

When I remember that I am a good friend,
I have even more friends – a whole bunch!

I am a good friend! All the time, every time.
I am a good friend – that's me!

Thank you for reading this book to the child in your life!
We hope this helps them understand that they are and can be a
good friend all the time, every time!

If you enjoyed this book please leave a review on Amazon or Goodreads.
We want to hear what you think!

You can follow Belle on Amazon and stay up to date on new releases!
You can also follow her blog at www.authorbellegreen.com and
find her on Facebook as Author Belle Green.

Joyful World Press, 2018

Made in the USA
Middletown, DE
15 September 2023

38572180R00020